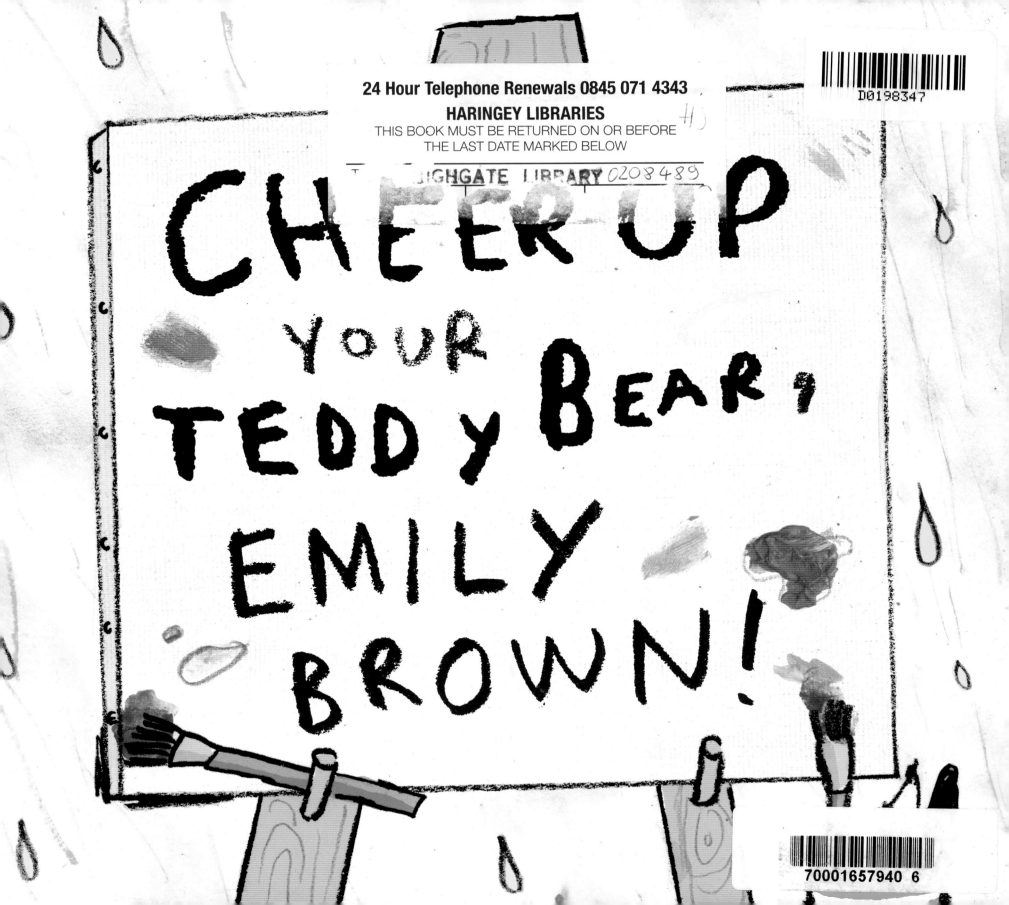

CHEER UP YOUR TEDDY BEAR, EMILY BROWN!

FOR SADIE AND ERICA - N.L.

FOR CLEMMIE COWELL - C.C.

First published in 2011

This paperback edition published in 2015

Text © Cressida Cowell 2011

Illustrations © Neal Layton 2011

Hodder Children's Books,

ISBN: 978 1 444 92342 1

338 Euston Road, London, NW1 3BH

Hodder Children's Books Australia,

Level 17/205 Kent Street, Sydney, NSW 2000

Hodder Children's Books is a division of Hachette Children's Books

An Hachette UK Company

www.hachette.co.uk

Printed in China

Cover designed by Jennifer Stephenson

CHEER UP YOUR TEDDY BEAR, EMILY BROWN!

written by
CRESSIDA COWELL

illustrated by
NEAL LAYTON

h
Hodder
Children's
Books

A division of Hachette Children's Books

Once upon a time,
there was a little girl called Emily Brown
and an old grey rabbit called Stanley.

One drippy, drizzly, wet weekend,
Emily Brown and Stanley were just building a camp in the
Outback of Australia, because it was too rainy to go outdoors,
when there was a **PLIP!PLOP!PLIP!PLOP!** noise
coming from the toybox.

PLIP!
PLOP!
PLIP!
PLOP!

EMILY
BROWN'S
TOY-
BOX

'Uh-oh,' said Emily Brown to Stanley,
'I think there could be something wet in there...'

There certainly was.

It was a very wet teddy bear, and she was singing a song to herself
in a sad little voice, which went something like this:

'Po-o-o-o-o-or ME. . .
po-o-o-o-o-oor ME. . .
Poor little sad little wet little ME. . . .
I'm a Lonely Only Bear
and I'm feeling very blue. . .'

'Come and have fun with us in Australia,' said Emily Brown.
'We're bound to find some bears there.'

'Thank you,' said the Tearful Teddy Bear,
'but there ARE no other teddy bears.
I'm the lonely, only one.'

So Emily Brown and Stanley and the Tearful Teddy Bear
went camping in the Outback of Australia.

And Emily Brown and Stanley were just as happy as could be, lighting campfires and spotting kangaroos and making friends with emus, and Emily Brown was just thinking, 'this will cheer up that Tearful Teddy Bear,' when there was a **PLIP! PLOP! PLIP! PLOP!** noise behind her…

…and it was the Tearful Teddy Bear, not cheered up at all.

PLIP PLOP! PLIP! PLOP!

'Oh dear,' said Emily Brown. 'Perhaps we should do something else.'

So Emily Brown and Stanley and the Tearful Teddy Bear
went walking in the big wild woods of Yellowstone Park.

And Emily Brown and Stanley had a very happy time
spotting small bears and large bears and black bears and grizzly bears
but absolutely no teddy bears.

And Emily Brown was thinking, 'this is a lot of fun,'
when there was a **PLIP!PLOP!PLIP!PLOP!** noise…

PLIP!
PLOP!
PLIP!
PLOP!

. . .and it was the Tearful Teddy Bear, gloomier than ever.

'Po-o-o-o-o-or ME. . .
po-o-o-o-o-oor ME. . .
Poor little sad little wet little ME. . .
I'm a Lonely Only Bear and I'm feeling very blue,
I've got no teddy friends and there's nothing here to do,
I'm bored and it's raining and raining is no fun. . .'

'Oh dear,' said Emily Brown.

'Maybe we should try something different.'

So Emily Brown and Stanley and the Tearful Teddy Bear
packed their paintbrushes and their easels and their most arty looking overalls
and went to paint sunflowers in the south of France.

And Emily Brown and Stanley had the most lovely time splashing swirls of glorious blue and yellow and red all over themselves, and Emily Brown was just thinking, 'this is the funn-est thing ever,' when there was a **PLIP!PLOP!PLIP!PLOP!** noise behind her…

. . . and it was the Tearful Teddy Bear, louder and sadder and more drippy than ever.

'Po-o-o-o-o-or ME. . .
po-o-o-o-o-oor ME. . .
Poor little sad little wet little ME. . .
I'm a Lonely Only Bear and I'm feeling very blue,
I've got no teddy friends and there's nothing here to do,
I'm bored and it's raining and raining is no fun,
There are no other teddy bears,
I'm the lonely
only one. . .'

And this time, her song was so sad,

and so loud,

and so miserable

that a TERRIBLE thing happened.

Emily Brown and Stanley began to feel quite sad, too,
and then the clouds spread and spread until they filled the sky and
they got bigger and blacker and drip drip drip the rain came down
and it looked like it was going to wash away the sunflowers.

'This has gone far enough,' said Emily Brown.
She took out her red umbrella and pointed it up at the sky…

With a lovely swooshing noise UP UP UP UP UP went Emily Brown's beautiful red umbrella.

'Wow…' whispered Stanley.

UP! went Emily Brown's umbrella and, leaping out of the sunflowers, came one, two, three, four, five, six, seven, eight, nine, ten, eleven, **TWELVE** little teddy bears, who had been having a picnic, but were all in a hurry to get out of the rain!

'I'm not the lonely only teddy bear after all!' said the Tearful Teddy Bear.

'We've been here all the time,' the teeniest of the teddy bears squeaked gruffly. 'And we'd really like you to join our picnic. But your song was so sad, we've been hiding.'

'I think,' said Emily Brown firmly, 'that it could be time for you to stop this sad song, and start smiling again.'

'Oh Emily Brown, Emily Brown,'
wept the Tearful Teddy Bear.

'You see, that's the real problem.
Someone has sewn my mouth
on upside down, and I'm not
sure that I CAN smile…'

'Why don't you TRY?' said Emily Brown.
'Think of happy things, and see if that works.'

So the Tearful Teddy Bear screwed up her teddy forehead and tried to smile as hard as she could. She thought of all the other teddy bears wanting to play with her and… **PING!** The left side of her mouth worked free of the stitches and waved happily in the wind.

And then she thought of the delicious picnic and… **PONG!**
The right side of her mouth unpicked itself and wriggled upwards
into a wibbly-wobbly smile. And a funny thing happened…

When the Tearful Teddy Bear smiled, the clouds got lighter and lighter, and the sun came out again and, as the very last raindrop dropped
PLOP!
onto the Cheerful Tearful Teddy Bear's head, all the little teddy bears sat down for a picnic in the sunflowers.

But Emily Brown and Stanley went outside
to play in the rain…

…and they got very, VERY wet.